The New Adventures of Postman Pat

Postman Pat™

in a muddle

John Cunliffe

Illustrated by Stuart Trotter

from the original television designs by **Ivor Wood**

*Hodder
Children's
Books*

a division of Hodder Headline plc

More Postman Pat adventures:

Postman Pat and the hole in the road
Postman Pat and the suit of armour

First published 1996
by Hodder Children's Books,
a division of Hodder Headline plc,
338 Euston Road, London NW1 3BH

Story copyright © 1996 Ivor Wood and John Cunliffe
Text copyright © 1996 John Cunliffe
Illustrations copyright © 1996 Hodder Children's Books
and Woodland Animations Ltd.

ISBN 0 340 678070
10 9 8 7 6 5 4 3 2 1

Printed in Italy.

It was a warm morning in Greendale, and there were plenty of letters and parcels for Pat to deliver. He was just finishing the village post, when he met Major Forbes. The Major was busy reading his paper, with his nose almost touching the page!

"Morning, Major!" called Pat.

"Morning, Pat! I say, this print gets smaller and smaller. Can't think what these fellows are up to! Can't see the half of it!"

"Well, now, Major," said Pat, "I couldn't read a thing without my glasses. It's ever so fuzzy and blurred without them. It might be that you need a pair."

"Oh, what a nuisance!" said Major Forbes. "I suppose I'll have to pop into Pencaster for an eye test. And you know me, Pat - always losing things . . . breaking things. My Aunt Penny sat on her glasses once - smashed them to bits! Very painful."

"You won't have to do that, Major!" said Pat. "Well, I'd best be on my way! Cheerio!"

"What would I do without my glasses?" said Pat to Jess.

At the post office, Mrs Goggins was busy sorting the letters.
"My goodness," said Pat, "what a hot day!"
He took his hat and his glasses off to wipe his face with a tissue.

"That's better!"

Then the doorbell jingled, and in came a big parcel,
with someone behind it.

"Hello, who's that?" said Pat.

It was Ted Glen.

"Catch hold of that corner, Pat," said Ted.
"It's a bit . . . oops . . . it's a right weight . . . oooh!"

Pat caught hold of the nearest corner.

"Just get it on there," gasped Ted. "That's it . . . PUSH!"

They heaved it higher, and dumped it on the counter.

"I hope it's nothing that breaks easily!" said Pat. "It went down with a bit of a thump."

"Nay, it'll be all right," said Ted. "I'm just glad to get it here all in one piece."

"Oh, Ted, what a monster!" said Mrs Goggins. "I can't be doing with this on my counter all morning! Just look at my letters - all flattened . . ."

"I rang Pencaster parcel office," said Ted, "and they said they'd pick it up just as soon as possible. Never you fear - they'll be here before you've had your cup of tea."

"Just look at the time!" said Pat. "I'd better be off!
Where did I put my hat? And where are my . . ."

"Erm . . . look under here, Pat," said Mrs Goggins, as she pulled
letters out from under the giant parcel. Ted lifted it up for her.
"Here we go . . . hup!"

"Don't drop it!" said Mrs Goggins. "I can feel something . . .
Oh . . . dear me . . ."

She had found a bent and crumpled something,
with bits of broken glass.

"Oh, Pat, is that your glasses?" said Ted.

"What's left of them," said Pat. "They're not much use now. How am I going to deliver these letters? I can't see to drive, never mind read the addresses."

"Now, Pat," said Mrs Goggins, "Ted can take you home in his lorry, and you can get your spare pair of glasses."

"What spare pair?" moaned Pat.

"Oh, Pat, haven't you got a spare pair?"

"No! I've never broken them before.
I've had these for years and years."

"Well," said Ted, "you'll have to borrow some."

"You can try my old ones," said Mrs Goggins. "They might do."

"If only I hadn't brought that parcel in . . ." said Ted. "Don't
worry, Pat, we can take the letters round in the lorry . . .
I can give you a hand."

"Thanks, Ted. I certainly won't be able to drive."

Mrs Goggins had found her old pair in a drawer.

"Here we are! Give these a try, Pat!"

"Oh, ummm . . . well . . . let's see . . ."

Pat screwed up his eyes, and looked round.

"Well, it's better than nothing . . . still a bit fuzzy . . .
I'll manage . . ."

But he tripped over a mop and bucket on his way to the door.
"Ooops!"
"Deary, me!" said Mrs Goggins. "What next?"
"Don't worry," said Ted. "I'll keep an eye on him."
And he followed Pat, carrying his letters.

They met Dr Gilbertson, doing her shopping.
Pat was not sure who it was.

"Good morning . . . erm . . . um . . . getting hot, isn't it?" he said.
"Now, then, Dorothy, I've got lots of letters for you. This looks like
one of yours. Here we are - have a good read! It'll do wonders for your
milk-yield."

"Pat," Ted whispered in his ear,
"that's not Dorothy . . ."

"Oh? Oooh! Aaaah!" said Pat.

"Are you feeling ill, Pat?" said
Dr Gilbertson.

"I'm sorry, Doctor, it's my glasses . . .
squashed flat under a parcel."

"They don't look squashed to me!"

"These are your letters, Doctor,"
said Ted.

"Well I never, what is going on?"
said Dr Gilbertson.

"Better be on our way with
these letters," said Ted.

Pat and Ted went on their way in Ted's lorry.

The next stop was at the church.
The letters seemed to have become mixed up.
"Tell you what," said Ted. "We can let the tail-gate down, and we'll have a good place to sort them out - as good as Mrs Goggins' counter."
"I'll just deliver this lot, whilst you sort the rest," said Pat.
"Are you sure you've got all the Reverend's letters?" said Ted.
"I'd know them with my eyes shut - I've been delivering letters for more years than you've had hot dinners."

The Reverend Timms was kneeling on the lawn,
doing some weeding. Pat fell over him.
"Ooops! Jess! What are you doing there?"
"Good Lord deliver us, Pat," said the Reverend,
"I'm not Jess. What are you doing?
You are Pat, aren't you? Sorry, Pat,
I've got the wrong glasses on . . .
can't see you properly . . .
all right for the weeding, but not for faces.
Bless me, where did I put my proper glasses?"
"I know just how you feel, Reverend," said Pat.
"I've got Mrs Goggins' old glasses on."
"Did you say Mrs Goggins . . .?"
"Yes, but it's a long story - have some letters.
I'd better be on my way, Reverend," said Pat,
looking at a Timms-shaped bush.
"By the way, your hair's looking a bit green -
must be this hot weather. Cheerio!"

Ted was holding out a postcard to Pat.

"*This* is for the Reverend, Pat! I think you've got them muddled again."

The Reverend Timms followed Pat to the gate, looking very puzzled.

"Pat, these are not for me at all. The writing's a bit fuzzy, but I do believe it says 'Miss Hubbard' on this one."

"You'll have to excuse him, Reverend," said Ted. "It was my fault, partly. You see, his glasses were squashed flat . . ."

"They look all right to me," said the Reverend Timms.

"It's a long story . . ." said Pat, "and I think it'll be best if you read out all the addresses for me, from now on, Ted."

"No problem!" said Ted.

"I wish I could help," said the Reverend, "but I don't know what's become of my proper glasses. They're in the lap of the gods. It's my memory, you know . . . it gets worse and worse. I *wonder* where I put them?"

"It's nice of you to offer to help," said Pat. "Thanks, Reverend, and cheerio!"

"Bye, Pat!"

Off went Ted and Pat, to the school.
"They seem to have moved the gate," said Pat.
"It was here yesterday."
"I'll just pop in with this parcel," said Ted.

One of the children came to talk to Pat.

"Hello, Sarah," said Pat. "How's your dad?"

"Oooh, Pat, hello . . ." said the fuzzy shape.
"I'm not Sarah, I'm Lucy."

"Oh dear, what a muddle!" said Pat. "Sorry about that!
What a silly thing to do. Ask Ted. He'll tell you . . ."

Mr Pringle came to see Pat.

"Now then, Ted," said Pat. "Let's not dally - we have such a lot
of letters to deliver."

"Oh, Pat," said Mr Pringle, "what a joker you are!
Ted's told me all about your glasses, but surely I'm not all that fuzzy?"

"Oh, sorry, Mr Pringle . . . it's awful, I really did think
you were Ted."

"Come on, Pat," said Ted.

They were on their way. The next stop was at Thompson Ground.

"There's Alf's catalogue," said Ted. "Now you can't go wrong with that!"

Pat went to look for Alf. His glasses were so fuzzy that he thought he could see Alf, sitting on his tractor.

"Are you there, Alf?"

The tractor did not reply.

"Alf?"

Pat stubbed his toes on the tractor's wheels.

"Oh dear, talking to a tractor, now. Sorry, tractor. I don't suppose you want a catalogue? Dear me, but Alf can't be far away. Anybody in?"

Pat felt his way out round the farm buildings. He found a large

letterbox, and popped the catalogue into it.

When he went back to the lorry, Ted said, "Did you find Alf, then?"

"He wasn't about," said Pat. "I just popped it in their new letterbox."

"New letterbox?" said Ted. "They haven't got a new letterbox."

"See for yourself," said Pat.

Ted went to look.

"It was somewhere round here," said Pat, but he could not find the door, never mind the letterbox. Then, at last . . . "Here we are! Didn't I tell you? A new letterbox."

"An old barn door with a missing plank, more like," said Ted. "Locked up as well. Now, then, how are we going to get it back? Hang on - I'll get someone to help us."

"Let's have a look," said Pat.
"If only I could see properly . . ."
Pat walked into a ladder.

"Ouch!"
Then he decided to climb it.
"Where does this go? I could get in through the window," he said to himself.
It led into the hayloft over the barn.

"Anybody there?"

Pat thought he could see Alf, standing in a dark corner.

"What are you doing up here, Alf?" said Pat. "Oh, no, it's an old coat! Well, it could do with a new outfit from that catalogue! Where is everybody?"

Suddenly, Pat disappeared! He had fallen through the trap-door, on to the pile of hay below. Luckily, he had a soft landing.

Ted came looking for Pat,
outside the locked barn door.
"Pat! Where are you?"
He could hear Pat blundering
about in the darkness inside.
"Sounds like a mad bull."
Alf Thompson came at last.
"Hello, Ted. Having a nice talk to my barn door?"
"Hello, Alf. Nay, I'm talking to Pat."
"Well, how's he got in there?" said Alf. "It's all locked up.
We'll have a look, if I've got the right key."

They found Pat, covered in hay, and holding the crumpled catalogue in his hand.

"Well, I'll be bothered, Pat, how ever did you get in there . . ." said Alf. "And just look at you!"

They dusted Pat down, and Dorothy served them all a pot of tea with fresh scones, and Pat soon felt himself again.

When all the letters had been delivered,
Ted took Pat back to the post office.
    "Oh, Ted and Pat, back at last!" said Mrs Goggins.
"I've been ringing round everywhere, trying to track you down!"
    "Now then, Mrs Goggins, there's no need to worry about us,"
said Pat. "It's been a long day, and a hot one, but we managed,
somehow. There's nothing else gone wrong, has there?"
    "Oh, no, Pat, it's just that after you'd gone,
I found these . . . they look awfully like yours."
    She showed Pat a pair of glasses.

"They must have slipped down behind the stamp book . . . that huge parcel must have given them a push."

"Let's try them," said Pat. "Magic! I can see again! Oh, that's lovely! They must be mine. Thank you, Mrs Goggins - thank you so much."

"Hang on," said Ted. "We saw them all smashed up."

"No, we didn't!" said Mrs Goggins. "There must have been another pair of glasses on the counter."

"Whose could they be?" said Pat.

"Well," said Mrs Goggins. "The Reverend came in
before you this morning, and he must have left his glasses here.
Miss Hubbard was talking to him, ten to the dozen . . .
that would make anyone forget anything. He popped in again,
after you called on him. He didn't mind about his glasses being broken.
Said he needed a new pair anyway. The old ones were for ever sliding
down his nose, and muddling him up in the middle of a service,
so he's gone off to Pencaster for a new pair."

"Well, I never," said Ted. "I wonder if I need glasses?
I think I'll invent a pair that never gets lost. Back to the workshop!
What a long hot day it's been."

"The post would never have got through without you," said Pat.
"Thanks, Ted. Oh, and can I order a pair of your un-lose-able glasses?
Cheerio!"

"And another pair for the Reverend!" said Mrs Goggins.
"Bye, Pat . . . Bye, Ted!"